MERCER MAYER'S CRITTER KIDS® ADVENTURE #1



# THE SWAMP THING

## A GRAPHIC NOVEL ADVENTURE

SOMETHING IS MOVING OUT THERE!



School Specialty. Publishing


Published by School Specialty Publishing, a member of the School Specialty Family.
A Big Tuna Trading Company, LLC/J. R. Sansevere Book

Written by Erica Farber/J. R. Sansevere

ISBN 0-7696-4762-6

1 2 3 4 5 6 7 8 9 10 PHX 11 10 09 08 07 06

Mr. Hogwash and the Critter Kids were going on a class trip to Snake Hill Swamp Sanctuary. They were going to learn all about life in a swamp.

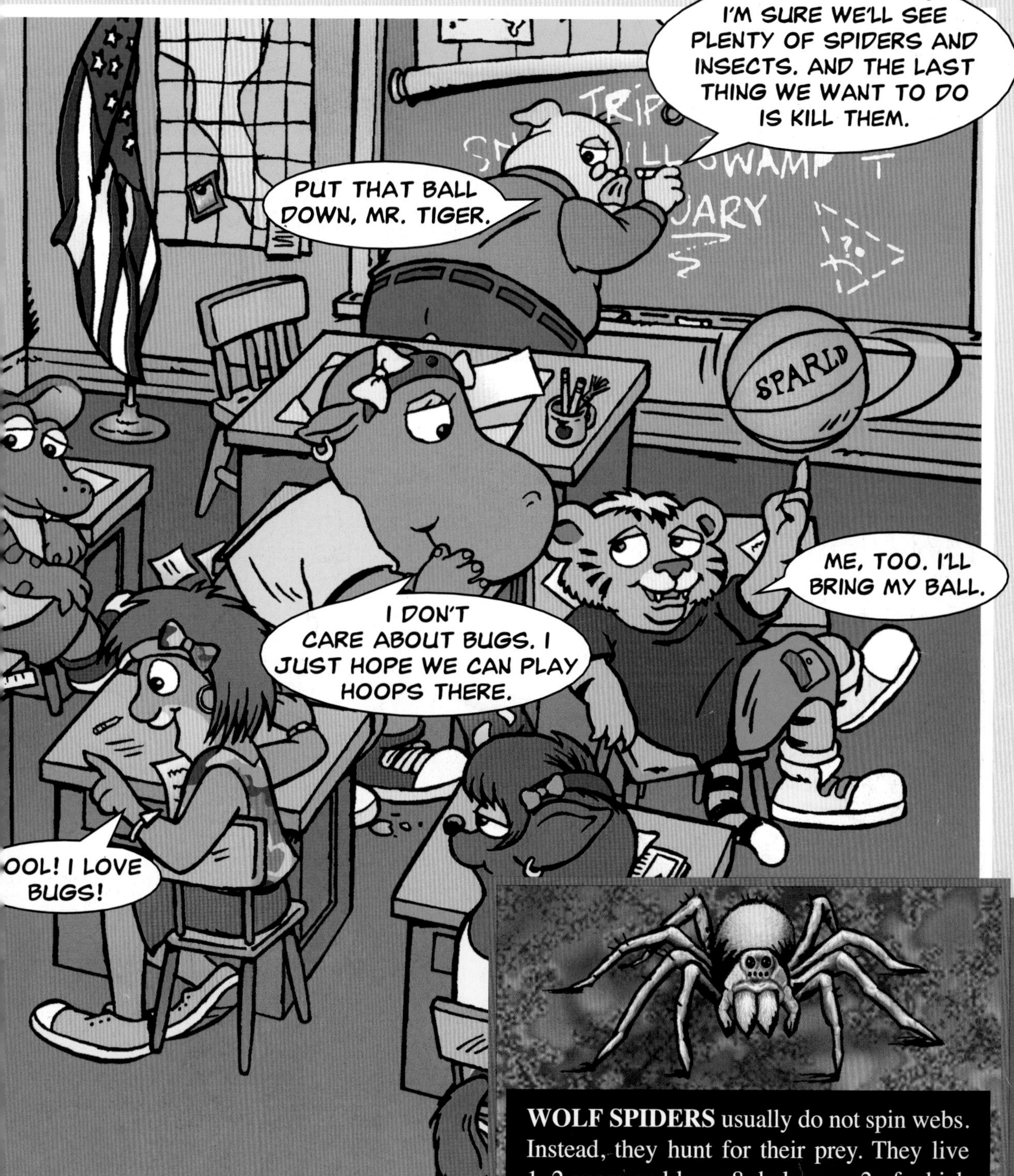
I'M SURE WE'LL SEE PLENTY OF SPIDERS AND INSECTS. AND THE LAST THING WE WANT TO DO IS KILL THEM.
OOL! I LOVE BUGS!
I DON'T CARE ABOUT BUGS. I JUST HOPE WE CAN PLAY HOOPS THERE.
ME, TOO. I'LL BRING MY BALL.
PUT THAT BALL DOWN, MR. TIGER.
SPARLD

**WOLF SPIDERS** usually do not spin webs. Instead, they hunt for their prey. They live 1–2 years and have 8 dark eyes, 2 of which are on top of their heads (not pictured).

After school, LC went home to pack for his trip. Little Sister gave him her spear shooter—just in case the Swamp Thing came to get him.

**BINOCULARS** are like 2 telescopes put side by side. You can see farther with a telescope, but binoculars let you can see more clearly because you can use both eyes.

HMMMM.

DANGER
GENIUS AT
WORK

ISN'T THAT SWEET, DEAR?

HERE'S MY SPEAR SHOOTER. IT'S GOOD FOR GETTING MONSTERS LIKE THE SWAMP THING.

CAN'T FORGET THIS.

The next morning, the Critter Kids left for Snake Hill Swamp. After driving for a long time, they finally entered the wetlands.

FOSSILS are impressions or pieces of plants or animals from long ago that died and got buried in mud, sand, or shells. Over time, the impressions turned into rock.

When they got to Snake Hill Swamp Sanctuary, the Critter Kids followed Mr. Hogwash to the visitors' center to meet Mrs. Pringle, their guide. She told them that the sanctuary was dedicated to preserving wildlife in their natural habitats.

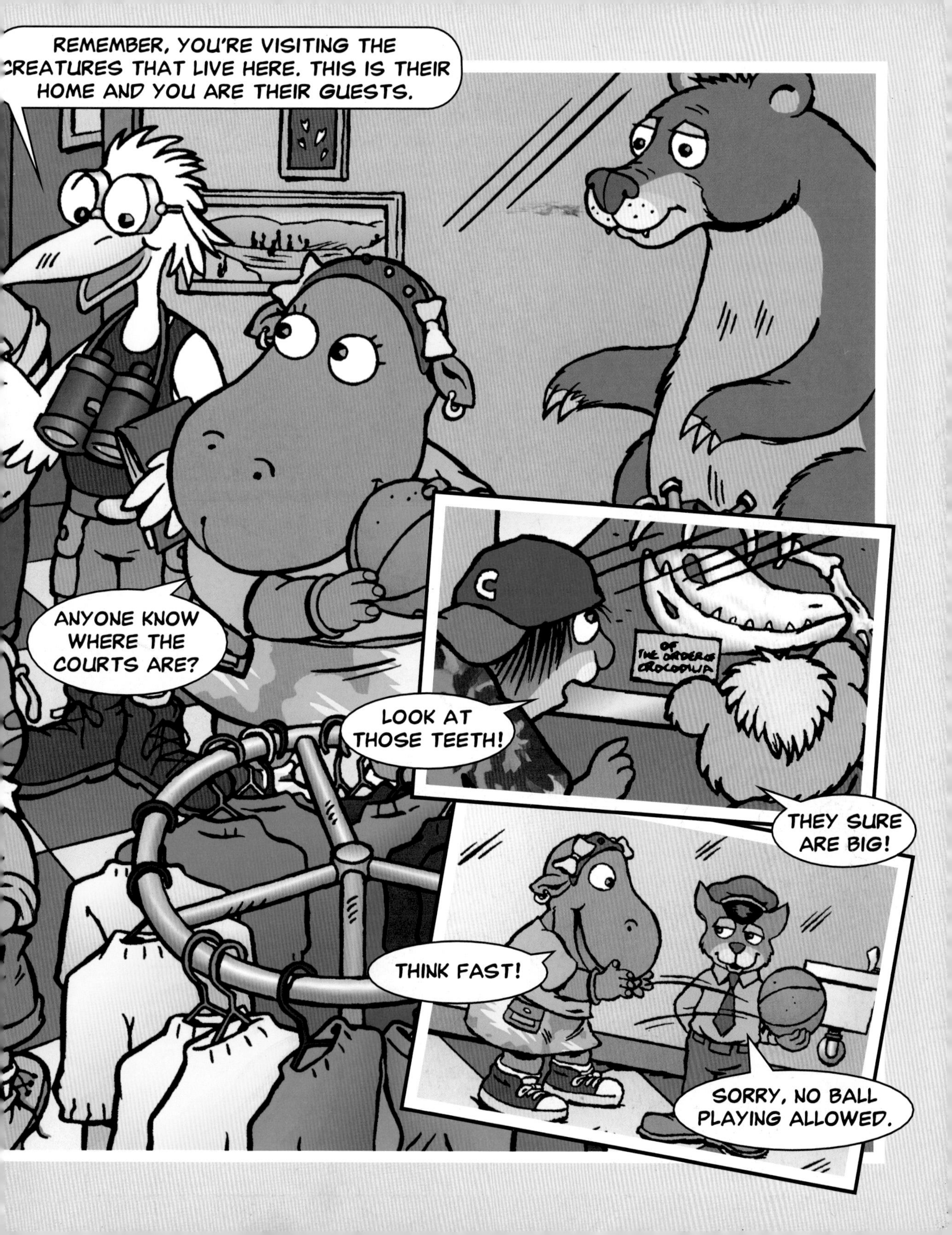
REMEMBER, YOU'RE VISITING THE CREATURES THAT LIVE HERE. THIS IS THEIR HOME AND YOU ARE THEIR GUESTS.
ANYONE KNOW WHERE THE COURTS ARE?
LOOK AT THOSE TEETH!
THEY SURE ARE BIG!
THINK FAST!
SORRY, NO BALL PLAYING ALLOWED.

Mrs. Pringle, Mr. Hogwash, and the Critter Kids all walked out to the boardwalk. Mrs. Pringle's son, Roger, showed them his pet snake.

All **SNAKES** have a poor sense of hearing and sight. However, some snakes have heat detector pits that allow them to sense another animal—even in the dark!

**GREEN ANOLES** can quickly change from green to brown, which makes them hard to find. If you catch one by the tail, don't think you've got it. It will just drop off its tail and run away. Don't worry—a new tail will grow.

CAN YOU DO MY BACK?

LIZARDS EAT BUGS FOR FOOD. IF THEY DIDN'T, BUGS WOULD TAKE OVER THE WORLD.

HOW ABOUT SOME BUG SLIME FOR YOUR BACK?

SAVE THAT BUG— THE LIZARD'S ABOUT TO GET IT!

IT'S KNOWN AS THE FOOD CHAIN.

Everybody walked far out on the boardwalk until they were completely surrounded by trees, plants, and creatures. The Critter Kids were all looking around, except for Su Su—she just wanted to sunbathe.

**LUBBER GRASSHOPPERS** are large and can't fly. If you catch one, hold your nose! When handled, lubbers give off a foul smell. Their spiny back legs can also cut your skin.

SOME OF THE FINEST BIRDS LIVE HERE.

OH, REALLY?

ICK! GET IT AY FROM ME!

HELLO, DOWN THERE.

ISN'T THAT A PRETTY BIRD?

Only female **MOSQUITOES** will bite you, because they need blood to lay their eggs. They are attracted to the warmth and moisture of your skin.

LC spotted something strange through his binoculars. Roger told him that it might be the Swamp Thing. LC leaned over the rail to get a better look. Suddenly, he fell right into the water!

Put a **DROP OF POND WATER** under a microscope, and you will see algae and lots of tiny animals.

That night, the Critter Kids roasted marshmallows around the campfire. And Roger told them about the Swamp Thing that lived at Snake Hill Swamp.

The **SOUTHERN BULLFROG** is also called the "pig frog" because its croak sounds like snorting. It uses its sticky, forked tongue to catch insects and worms.

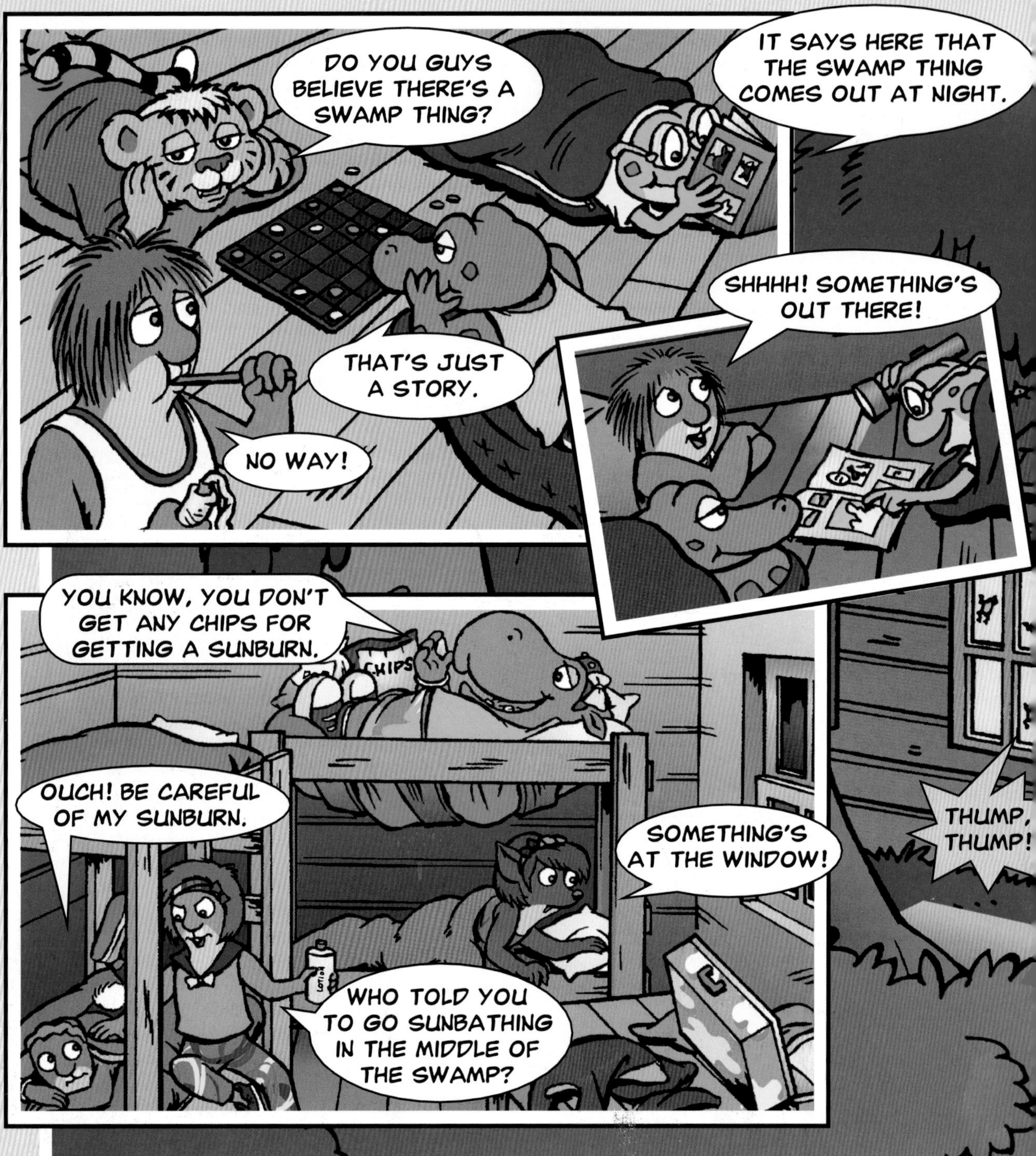
DO YOU GUYS BELIEVE THERE'S A SWAMP THING?
IT SAYS HERE THAT THE SWAMP THING COMES OUT AT NIGHT.
THAT'S JUST A STORY.
NO WAY!
SHHHH! SOMETHING'S OUT THERE!
YOU KNOW, YOU DON'T GET ANY CHIPS FOR GETTING A SUNBURN.
CHIPS
OUCH! BE CAREFUL OF MY SUNBURN.
WHO TOLD YOU TO GO SUNBATHING IN THE MIDDLE OF THE SWAMP?
LOTION
SOMETHING'S AT THE WINDOW!
THUMP, THUMP!

The Critter Kids went back to their cabins to get ready for bed. Suddenly, they heard the strangest sounds. There was something outside their windows! Everybody thought it was the Swamp Thing, but it was just a bunch of frogs.

**GREEN TREE FROGS** can change color from green to gray. They have toe pads that grip like suction cups, and can attach themselves to plants or even windows.

The next morning, Mrs. Pringle took the Critter Kids on a canoe ride. They were looking for her favorite bird— the wood stork.

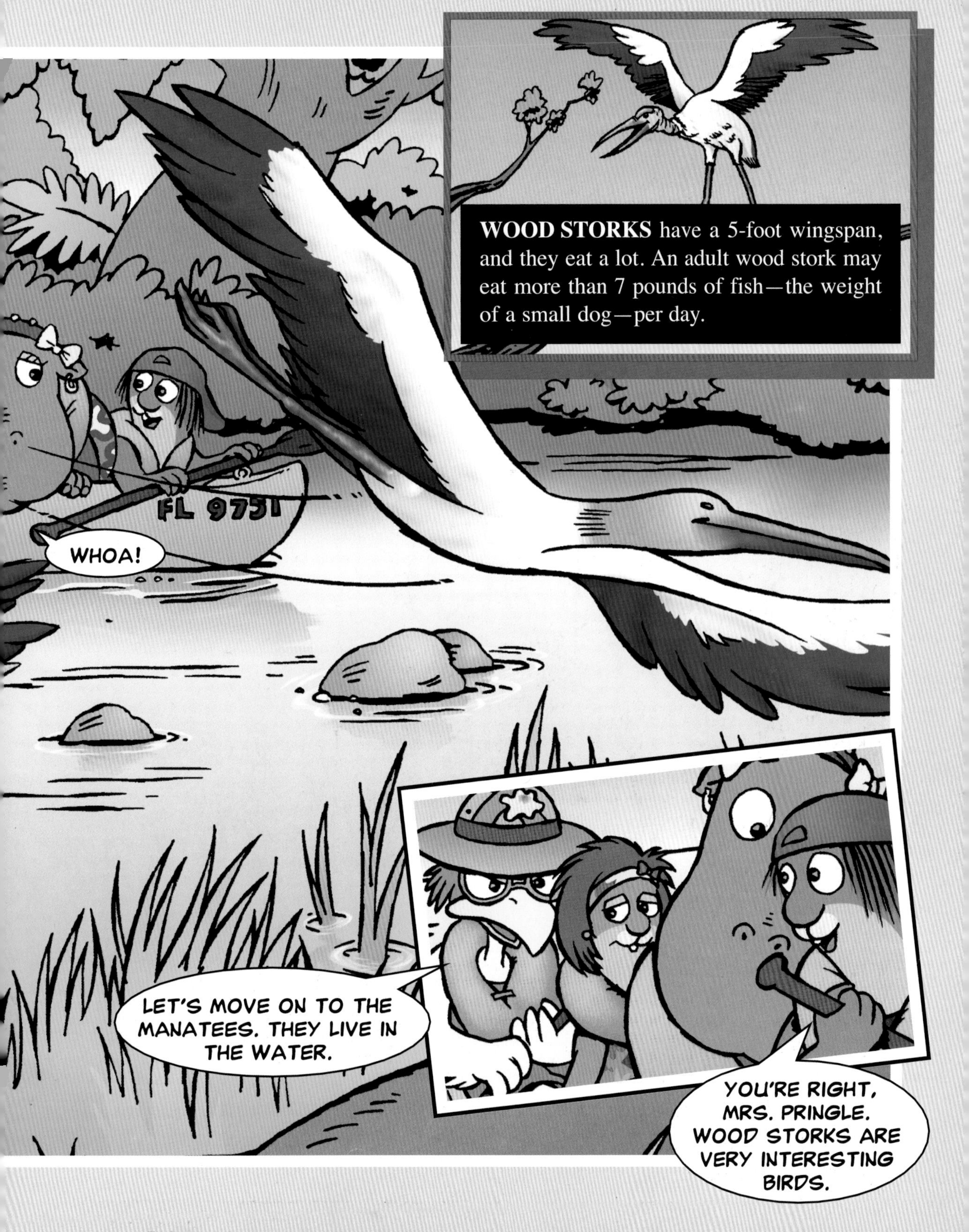

WOOD STORKS have a 5-foot wingspan, and they eat a lot. An adult wood stork may eat more than 7 pounds of fish—the weight of a small dog—per day.
FL 9731
WHOA!
LET'S MOVE ON TO THE MANATEES. THEY LIVE IN THE WATER.
YOU'RE RIGHT, MRS. PRINGLE. WOOD STORKS ARE VERY INTERESTING BIRDS.

Everybody canoed into a bay to see the manatees. Mrs. Pringle told them that manatees are endangered. One of their biggest threats is motorboats that run over them by accident.

An average-sized adult **MANATEE** weighs around 1000 pounds and eats about 60 pounds of vegetation a day! The manatee is a distant relative of the elephant.

After dinner, the Critter Kids sat on the porch and watched the sunset. Roger dared them to go to the swamp late that night to see the Swamp Thing.

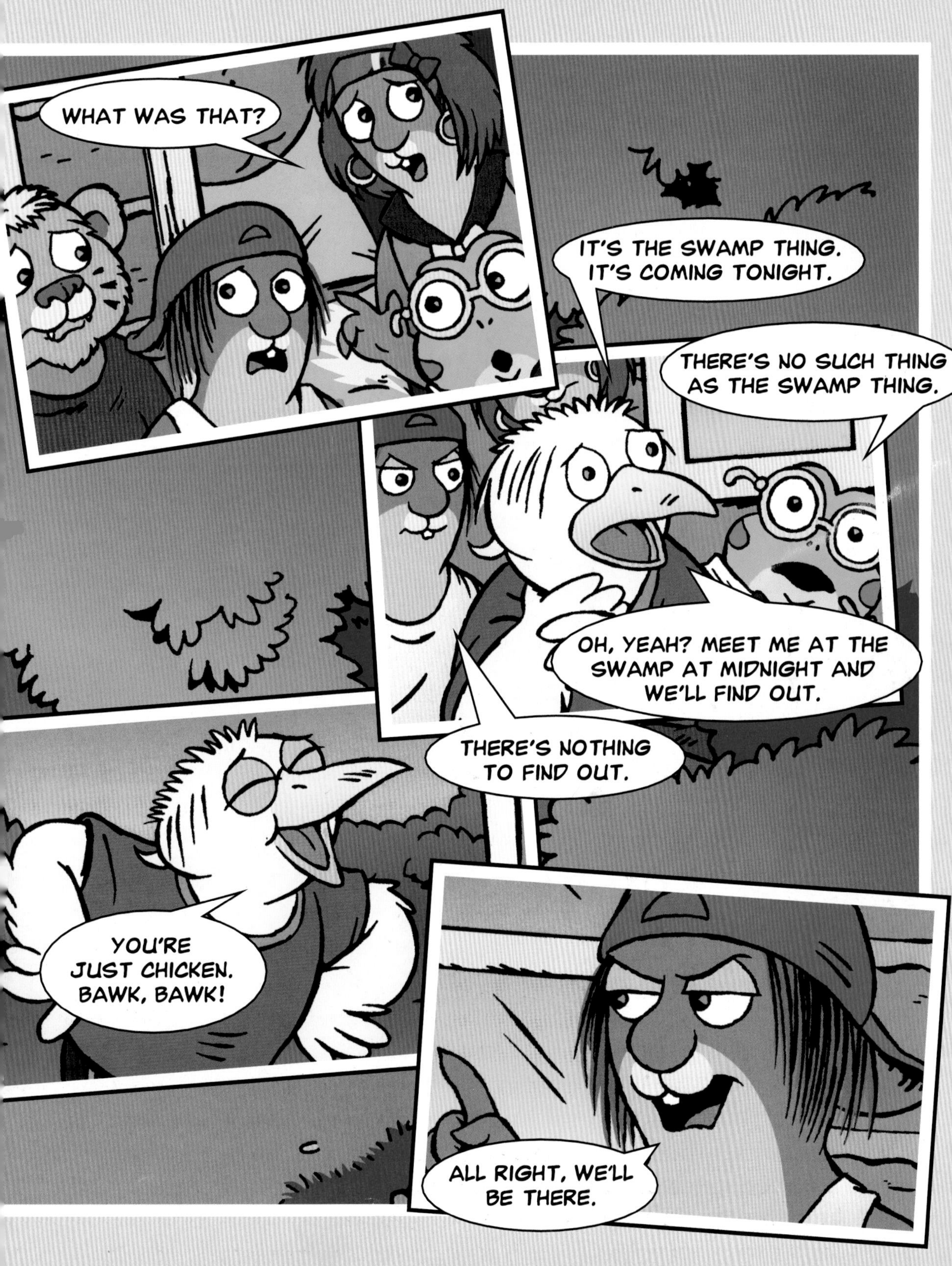
WHAT WAS THAT?
IT'S THE SWAMP THING. IT'S COMING TONIGHT.
THERE'S NO SUCH THING AS THE SWAMP THING.
OH, YEAH? MEET ME AT THE SWAMP AT MIDNIGHT AND WE'LL FIND OUT.
THERE'S NOTHING TO FIND OUT.
YOU'RE JUST CHICKEN. BAWK, BAWK!
ALL RIGHT, WE'LL BE THERE.

At the stroke of midnight, the Critter Kids followed Roger into the swamp. LC knew there was no such thing as the Swamp Thing. But he couldn't help thinking that if there were, it would definitely live in Snake Hill Swamp.

When you see **LIGHTNING**, count the number of seconds until you hear thunder. Then you will know how many miles away the lightning is (5 seconds = 1 mile).

Roger called the Swamp Thing. Suddenly, two big eyes popped out of the water just as Roger slipped and fell. LC grabbed the spear shooter that Little Sister had given him. The Critter Kids had to save Roger before the Swamp Thing got him!

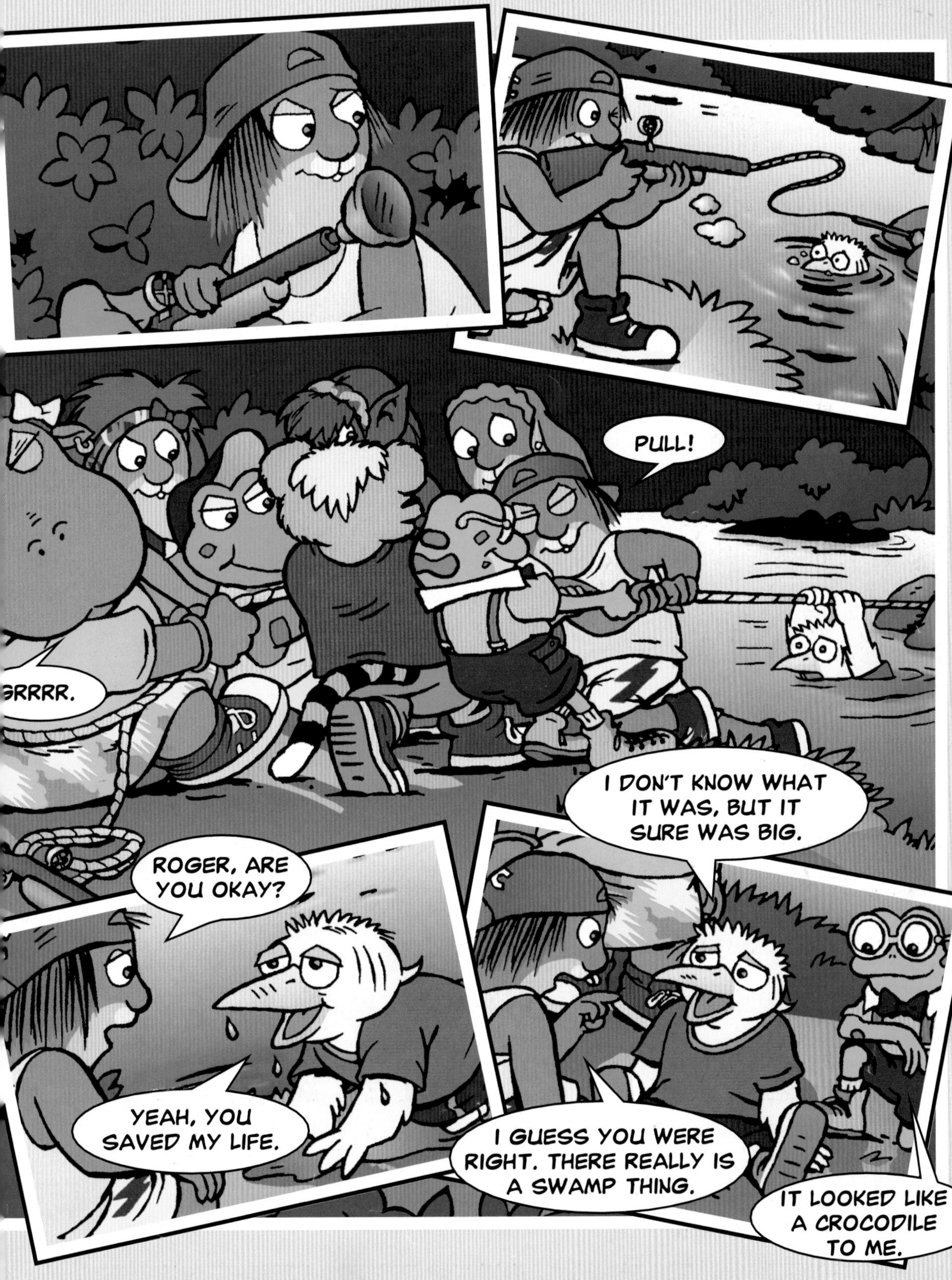
PULL!
GRRRR.
ROGER, ARE YOU OKAY?
YEAH, YOU SAVED MY LIFE.
I DON'T KNOW WHAT IT WAS, BUT IT SURE WAS BIG.
I GUESS YOU WERE RIGHT. THERE REALLY IS A SWAMP THING.
IT LOOKED LIKE A CROCODILE TO ME.

The next day, the Critter Kids went home. Mr. Hogwash gave LC a bag full of green chips. He had won the prize! All he had to do was go to Critter Comics and pick it up from Mr. Marvel.

CROCODILES are descendants of a large and ancient group of reptiles that existed in the time of dinosaurs.

# Vocabulary

**algae**—a plantlike organism that grows in a swamp. *The pond was full of green, brown, and red algae.*

**cycle**—a series of events that occur regularly or systematically. *A butterfly's cycle is egg, caterpillar, pupa, and adult butterfly.*

**endangered**—in danger of becoming extinct. *The manatee is an endangered animal that swims in shallow water, such as swamps, where it is often run over by motor boats.*

**habitat**—a place where plants and animals normally live. *Frogs usually live in a wet habitat.*

**sanctuary**—a protected place. *The birds and animals of Snake Hill Swamp lived in a sanctuary where there was no danger of anyone hurting them.*

**specimen**—something set aside to be used for testing. *Timothy collected swamp water to be used as a specimen for his science project about algae.*

**vegetation**—a thick covering of plants. *The forest was overrun with vegetation.*

**wetlands**—a swampy or marshy area of land often covered with shallow water. *Cattails and other marsh plants grow well in the wetlands.*

# The Story and You

Name three animals that the Critter Kids saw on their trip. Which one do you think was the most interesting? Why?

What was the Swamp Thing? How do you know?

It took help from all of the Critter Kids to rescue Roger. Describe a time when you were part of a group effort to help someone.